Euphoric Vendetta
a thriller

Kajari Guha

Ukiyoto Publishing

All global publishing rights are held by
Ukiyoto Publishing
Published in 2024

Content Copyright © Kajari Guha

ISBN 9789362699794

All rights reserved.

No part of this publication may be reproduced, transmitted, or stored in a retrieval system, in any form by any means, electronic, mechanical, photocopying, recording or otherwise, without the prior permission of the publisher.

The moral rights of the author have been asserted.

This is a work of fiction. Names, characters, businesses, places, events, locales, and incidents are either the products of the author's imagination or used in a fictitious manner. Any resemblance to actual persons, living or dead, or actual events is purely coincidental.

This book is sold subject to the condition that it shall not by way of trade or otherwise, be lent, resold, hired out or otherwise circulated, without the publisher's prior consent, in any form of binding or cover other than that in which it is published.

www.ukiyoto.com

To my family and friends, especially my grand daughter, Sudeeksha!

Contents

Chapter-1   1

Chapter-2   4

Chapter-3   8

Chapter-4   11

Chapter-5   21

Chapter-6   25

Chapter-7   26

About the Author   **48**

Chapter-1

Twilight it was! The tranquil ambience of her balcony and a moment of quiet reflections! Yes! Finally her dream came true, the dream that she had cherished from her childhood! The whispering vendetta against those who spoilt her family life had invigorated her determination to mete out punishment to the culprits. The goal had been achieved, Shilpa felt euphoric, with a heightened sense of satisfaction, a surge of enthusiasm and energy, or a feeling of being on top of the world.

Shilpa was enjoying the cool breeze, cradling a steaming cup of tea in her hands, after the heavy downpour. Wisps of steam like her curly hair, rose delicately from the cup, the aroma enhanced, mixing the earthly scent of the wet soil. The warm sunlight embraced her. Its gentle shadows danced across her sharp features, illuminating the subtle contemplation that reflected in her eyes. The droplets woke up delicately on the leaves. They glistened like precious jewels in the soft sunlight as if breaking through the dissipating clouds. The blades of grass were parched and weary. They stood tall and vibrant after the shimmering raindrops supported them, quenching their thirst and reviving their verdant splendour. The soft rustle of leaves and the far-off chirping of birds provided a soothing soundtrack to Shilpa's solitude. She plunged into the simple pleasure of this tranquil moment, finding solace and serenity in the delicate balance of tea and introspection.

It had all begun with a determination when she lost her Papa. She couldn't forget the incidents that led to the most horrific experiences she had to deal with. From that very day she fought to bring the offenders to justice intensified, fuelled by the resolute commitment to shield those silenced by adversity.

The dimly lit conference room of the crime investigation department had been an witness to Inspector Shilpa Sen's tenacity and perseverance. With her sharp mind and keen intuition, she broke the barriers of a male dominated world. Clad in her uniform, she earned a lot of respect from her authority and colleagues. Her presence in the force inspired the women-folks to aspire for law enforcement, proving that gender can't be an obstacle to success. She used to sit engrossed in the files of daunting cases. The investigation into a fake drug trafficking and a suspected child abuse ring had consumed her thoughts and energy for months. The cases that shrouded the darkness of the innocent victims had pushed her to the brink of exhaustion.

One of the cases started with a single tip-off—a sudden phone call to Sumana Das, a pretty young woman in her forties. Destiny played its role and her husband, a tall handsome young man in his late forties, met with an accident decades ago that snatched away most comforts of his life. Then she had to join the administrative sector of a renowned educational institution of Kolkata. Their only child Triparna, naturally, was the apple of her eyes. However, in the short span of her life,Triparna had seen many things that made her more mature than any other girl of her age. She was an adorable child, especially for her Papa with whom she shared everything.It was the Monday morning, hectic with the rushing footsteps and hurried greetings, keyboards clicking and coffee cups clinking, when she received the call.

"Hello! I am CBI commissioner. Am I speaking to Mrs.Das?"

"Yes"!Sumana was completely taken aback after hearing the next sentences.

"Do you know anything about your daughter, Triparna? She hired a cab.That cab was carrying twenty kilos of cocaine. So your daughter has been arrested as she was sitting in the same car. If you wish to recover her from this untoward situation, come near Chandni chowk police station with fifty thousand rupees."

Sumana was all mixed up. She recalled the incident that happened with her daughter a year ago when she went to Goa with her friends.

"Hasn't she learnt a lesson? How can it be? Triparna should be in her class now, attending psychology lectures in Amity University. O my Goodness !She is everything in my life. How can I protect her from these tyrants? What shall I do if something happens to her?"she thought.

A barrage of questions got triggered in her mind. Triparna, a smart confident girl of nineteen years was blooming like a rose. Her ivory complexion adorned with beautiful black curly hair was a heartthrob for many. Her sharp features with eyes like pools of liquid amber, shimmered with a captivating depth. They held the untold mysteries of the universe within their gaze speaking volumes without uttering a word. An inner radiance reflected in her eyes. She had the underlying wisdom far beyond her years. Is she safe?

Sumana didn't answer the call and phoned her daughter straight away.

"Hello Tiru ! Where are you?"

"Why Mom? Where can I be except in my class?"

"Please let me have a glimpse of yours. Please switch on your video."

"Ok".

Triparna switched on the video on her cell phone and the worried mother heaved a sigh of relief. She informed the nearby police station immediately.

Acting swiftly, Shilpa and her team launched a covert surveillance operation.

It was a network of criminals preying on the most defenceless members of the society, exploiting their innocence for personal gain. These types of cases about drug trafficking and Child abuse or abduction for ransom, a multifaceted issue, are manifested in various forms across the country. Cases of sexual assault often go unreported due to fear, shame and trauma making it impossible for the victims to come forward and resolve the issue.

Shilpa could not abstain from delving deeper into the past. How could she forget about Riya, a young victim of child abuse leading to trauma and the shattering of the bonding between her parents?

Shilpa was lost somewhere, peeping into her childhood experiences.

Chapter-2

It was years ago when Surabhi asked Shilpa to unpack her small rucksack.

"Why Ma?"

"Did you take your sketchpad?"

"How many times will you ask?"

"And what about Sona's tennis racket… ? Has he packed it?

You must check Shilpa. You are his elder sister."

"Please Ma don't be scary. Everything's ready."Shilpa had answered. The cab had arrived. Shilpa's Papa carried the suitcase downstairs. Shilpa and Sona took hold of the two light-weight bags. In those days, the domestic airlines did not allow more than fifteen k.gs. per passenger travelling by Economy class. Surabhi locked the doors and boarded the cab.

The vacation had started. They never had a chance to take a flight. Shilpa and her little brother Sona were too excited. Above all, the place they were going to visit was Nature's haven, where Nature speaks in its own language.

Surabhi recalled Mrs.Roy's comments.

"You can't even guess how relaxing it was! We lit the camp fire, sang and danced and so on…"her stories went by.

"Surabhi…you must do something this year."She said to herself and her wishes were fulfilled by God's grace.

Rajan and Surabhi, Shilpa's parents, were married for long. Surabhi, a loyal and sincere teacher in a renowned school, always had a petty penchant for seeing the far-off places.It was dormant in her mind, but Rajan would never like to spend a farthing extra. Every time he went on planning a safe and secure future for his family.

"Su, where have you kept the file for LIC and Mutual funds?"would be the usual question after coming back from his bank.

"A crazy calculator!"Surabhi would murmur.This time they were lucky to win a contest and were able to plan the trip. The dream vacation was now on its way. They were to visit Andaman and Nicobar.

The formalities were done. They boarded safely, had fastened their seatbelts and Sona started peeping into Surabhi's handbag.

"Ma please give me the packet of chips."

"No Sona! Later! No fuss Ok?"

"Don't be so cross with the child Su, let them enjoy. We are going on a pleasure trip, aren't we?"said Rajan.

"You're just spoiling them."Surabhi frowned, but handed over the packet to Sona.

"Take. Don't finish them all. Share it with your Didi."

Sona had the window-seat. Shilpa felt a bit jealous. However Surabhi sat with them and Rajan had to sit in the next row. All four of them were thrilled. The children were buzzing with energy and settled into their seats. The engines roared, their faces lit up with excitement,their hearts racing with the sheer joy of newfound adventure. The airhostess locked the door. She showed how to fasten the seatbelt and what to do in case of emergency exit. One of the passengers who had a turban on his head, interrupted,

"Ma'am can I open the emergency exit just now to find out if it works?"

Everyone roared with laughter.

Shilpa laughed heartily recalling the incident.

The young beautiful girl explained the process once more. They were asked to switch off the phone. Surabhi and Rajan did so. Surabhi was trying to hide the phone. It was infra dig in a world of glamour and show-off not to possess an I-phone. The captain announced that the plane was going to take off. Shilpa and Sona held their hands. Their faces, anxious and scared, beamed with smiles of relief when the plane moved a few minutes on the runway and soared high into sky. The clouds made way, sometimes turning blue and suddenly stretching into smoky grey.

Two of the cabin crews were serving water for free. They were also selling drinks and snacks. Surabhi had brought food packets from home. The packets were opened. They started munching the food. It would take two to three hours to reach Portblair. Their plane would arrive there at midnight. The bell-boy from the hotel they had booked would be there at Veer Savarkar Airport to receive them.

Two and half an hour passed in the blink of an eye. The plane was about to land. Once more the signs for fastening seatbelts were lit and the announcement about their arrival was made by the captain.

Finally the door was opened. The tourists came out of the plane and went towards the carousel no.two. Shilpa and Surabhi took hold of the bags. Rajan was waiting for the VIP suitcase they had bought for this trip only. Sona was completely captured by the scene of luggage, moving round and round like a toy train. Rajan snatched their suitcase and made it stand on its wheels, then pulled.

The driver from Sunshine hotel with the bell-boy was standing with a placard. Their names were written on it. It was easy for him to locate because they themselves headed towards him. Outside the airport was standing the Innova, a luxurious car to take them to the hotel. There was another fellow who joined them. He was a tourist from Turkey. They got acquainted and Rajan started the conversation. They got engaged in a vibrant conversation, bridging the geographical gap and crossing the man made boundaries. The man from Turkey depicted the rich history of Istanbul's ancient landmarks.

"Have you ever tasted Turkish *kebabs* and *bakalava*? I think you would enjoy it." he said.

"Please drop in sometimes to our place, Kolkata. You would love the spicy *biryani* and *rasogolla*, the flavourful cuisine of our city." reacted Rajan.

The town looked very peaceful, far from the hectic din and bustle of daily life. They reached the hotel in a few minutes. Rajan shook hands with him and took care of his family.

All of them were speaking English. However, the people there knew Tamil, Telegu, Hindi, Bengali and Malayalam. They addressed India as Mainland.

The traditionally dressed waiters gave a warm welcome with a special drink made from coconut and banana, found there in abundance.

The food was delicious. Shilpa and Sona liked prawns, but their parents loved crabs. Children gorged. Surabhi warned them.

"Don't rush! You would be sick and the charm of the whole trip would be spoiled."

"Jai Hind Ma'am! We are ready to launch the raid.", the sub-inspector, Aruni, was standing in front of Shilpa. Aruni was young, brave and committed to the task she had been assigned. She was the right-hand of Shilpa. Beneath her stoic features lay a compassionate heart, dedicated to protect the vulnerable and to uphold the principles of justice and equality. She stood as a beacon of strength and integrity.

"Yes! Let us go."Shilpa's reverie broke, and she stood up from her chair.

Chapter-3

Sifting through the evidences in hand Shilpa tried to unfurl the pattern—a pattern of oppression, manipulation and intimidation. She started investigating Triparna's case and found the same gang connected with numerous child trafficking cases. She conducted a number of interviews with the victims. Most of them were young girls. Three of them left their homes in search of a glamorous life promised by their fiancé and kith and kin, but the life that culminated was like a nightmare they had never imagined. Seema, Meena and Salma, all three of them were about thirteen to fifteen years old.

Seema lived in Beldubi, located on the border of Panchla. Seema studied in class nine in Beldubi High school. She belonged to lower middle class. Her parents used to sell vegetables. Seema had a youthful vigour that made up for the emaciated body that might have been nourished only by rice and pulse one time a day, yet her enormous eyes dreamt of a life that would never allow her two siblings to cry everyday for a sumptuous meal. She made friends with Salim and he promised to connect her with the people offering a job in Kolkata that could fulfill her dreams. She escaped from her home with Salim who assured her to manage some kind of engagement that would let her earn in thousands in Kolkata. Salim took her to Tollygunj studio and handed her to the right hand of a producer who seduced her and never offered a role. One day Seema ran away from the place with the help of a sweeper and came to the police station.

Meena was beautiful. She was fair and tall. She had a rare elegance that seemed to transcend her poverty, but her step-father sold her to Hamid who was running a bar and was supplying girls to hotels. She was all at sea when she could detect the exact scenario. She was imprisoned in a dark room and was lucky enough to escape through the small window and sought shelter in the police station.

Salma used to stay in Bashirhaat, a place known for crimes. She was young and pretty. Her radiant smile illuminated her weary features, diffusing them with a sense of resilience and speaking of her inner strength. She was kidnapped by a gang,but was able to escape and report to police.

All these three were sheltered in the police station in a separate room where none except Shilpa had an access. She provided one of her most trusted associates to assist them in their daily chores. She knew that the criminals involved in these cases would try to kill them. She took extra care for them.

With each piece of information collected and interview conducted,she felt the responsibility weighing on her shoulders…a responsibility to seek justice for Riya and the others who had to keep mum, their cries unheard and drowned in the cacophony of the cruel criminal world. She pursued every step with caution patience and dogged determination.

In the meantime a luxury bus had become a sensation. It had been heading towards Wagah border. It was stopped near the checkpoint. The driver left and was absconding. When they asked the conductor to open the doors of the bus, he was in a dilly-dally. Shilpa asked her team to open the door forcefully. They arrested the conductor. The cops opened the door and what did they see?

About twenty cows instead of the passengers, were huddled up inside the Volvo luxurious bus.The case had been handed over to her colleague Kanishk Saxena as she was entangled with the child trafficking and drug smuggling case.

The next morning was Sunday, but there was no holiday for Shilpa. She hatched a plan to raid the blind-alley brothels with her team at night.

They reached there at 1 a.m. She checked all the rooms. The male draped in underpants and lungis scattered like pomegranate seeds and tried to escape, but most of them were caught. The girls were taken into custody, but the main culprit was not seen anywhere. A futile effort it was, yet Shilpa called the informer.

"Hello where are you? You bastard! Just fooled me? Meet me within an hour!"

"Ma'am! So sorry! Just a few minutes ago he left for Andaman and Nicobar island. He came to know about your raid."

"What…Andaman Nicobar?

Shilpa could hear something. Wasn't it her father ?

"Shilu…rush to Andaman."

Chapter-4

Sitting in the aircraft, the scenes from the past revisited her mind's eye. It was only a decade ago when Shilpa with her parents and younger brother had visited Andaman.

Located in the southern part of Andaman and Nicobar Islands Port Blair is known as the capital city and the municipal council of the islands. The aborigines actually had very less contact with the outside world. So they depended much on the seafood and fruits. They did not know about the use of fire for a long time. So they ate raw fish. Then many people from South India and other places had come there and settled. The place abounded with different kinds of cuisines and gastronomical urges of the tourists were fulfilled.

Shilpa recalled each and every moment. They had arrived in the hotel. After taking a nap they got ready to move towards the beaches. The palm trees were standing in a row to welcome the visitors. Shilpa and Sona started running on the beach. Surabhi and Rajan were strolling, enjoying the serenity of the setting sun. The glimmering touch of the dim golden light and the reddish tinge made the sun glow in the twilight. The children were scattered here and there. The girls were making friends with each other. The boys had formed a team and were playing football. All were in a happy-go-lucky mood, feeling free and safe. Dusk dropped in like a sudden unwelcome guest and the stars started twinkling, peeping through the dark velvety sky.

It was time to get back to the hotel, but before doing so they had to have their dinner. The hotel they were staying would not provide, so they walked towards the food stalls nearby that offered local cuisine.

All of a sudden Surabhi felt a hand on her shoulder. She turned back and found a face dazzling like the constellation, a beacon of beauty amidst the shady beach.

"Wow! What a pleasant surprise! Dear Ruby! Where had you been hiding for so long? I can't believe my eyes. Where is your best half?"

chuckled Surabhi. They used to call their better halves like that only. They thought they had the most docile husbands who could dance to their tunes.

"He is no more the best half. At present we don't like to see each other."Ruby replied.

"OMG! What's the story behind it?"Surabhi was filled with despair, love and above all, concern for her best friend.

"Mridul has completely changed. We are going to celebrate our twelfth anniversary this year and he is lost…lost and lost. Don't know what he's up to.

Every weekend he has some kind of excuse. He would leave the house in the afternoon on Saturday and come back late on Sunday evening. If I ask him, he creates a scene. He has unleashed least care for his daughter, Riya who is nine years old now."Ruby answered.

"Where is he? Has he come with you? And Riya? Where is she?"asked Surabhi.

"No, I have come alone to avail myself of my vacation. Riya would join me tomorrow. She is in a boarding school. One of my cousins is going to escort her." said Ruby.

"Fine.Let's have our dinner together." said Rajan finally who was listening to the whole story for about half an hour. They entered a roadside restaurant and took their seats. They planned their itinerary where to visit and when. Shilpa and Sona were exhilarated. They would get a company to play and talk to.

Next they moved towards their hotel, Ruby followed them. She was also staying in the same hotel.

Andaman glowed in the morning sunshine. The silver white sand on the palm-lined beach glimmered. Surabhi and the children came out of the room.The gorgeous sea with the sound of the waves lashing against the beach beckoned them. Surabhi stared at the vast infinity stretching against the horizon.

Nature has its own textures and flavours, Surabhi thought..No matter if it is the tempest or the smooth quiet sea, Nature stands tall to meet the challenges. "So are we!"reflected Surabhi. Ruby was still attractive in her forties. Was it anything else that trapped Mridul? Power, Pelf or Sex? She felt dizzy. Human mind is not a simple book to be read anywhere or everywhere. All the pages have different stories to tell.

The children jumped with joy when they met Riya, a pretty cute little girl with curly hair and large eyes, that looked blank. She was very quiet, quiet like an abandoned house. Shilpa held her hand and Sona tried to plunge into the depth of her stares and timid looks. Ruby and her cousin Somu insisted that Riya should mix with the children and should enjoy the beautiful ambience. But it was the other way round. Riya was just like a robot, lacking the spontaneity of a bubbling brook gushing and rushing wherever it could.

They had hatched a plan to visit Havelock and Neil Island. Those who were scared of swimming or diving had to leave the opportunity to experience the most exotic marine life with wonderful caches under the ocean. Surabhi, Shilpa and Sona were ready, but Rajan was in a dilemma.He had butterflies in his stomach. Surabhi knew what was going on in his mind. She held him close and asked him to stay back if he was feeling low. Ruby and Somu were also quite thrilled, but Riya? Large drops of tears rolled down her cheeks. She didn't utter a single word, but could not send the droplets back to their place.

"Come on Riya! Please cheer up. Don't get upset dear if you're not feeling well." reacted Ruby.

"Well ! Let's sit here together, Riya. Would you feel better with me? We would enjoy so many things here watching the beautiful show on the beach. Come on! Let them go."Rajan smiled.

Riya nodded after a long time.

Scuba diving was a new dimension for the tourists who visited Andaman. The amazing sea-life with colourful reefs and vast canyons allured them to unravel the mystery of the ocean. Light house that was six to twenty metres long with all levels was one of the famous dive-sites of Andaman.

Shilpa's joy knew no bounds. She had the adventurous spirit like her mother. Surabhi and Sona also were keen about it. Ruby and Somu liked the Wall dropping into the shipping channel,visited by the very friendly huge Napoleon Wrasse known as Pierre.

Like a wild electric current, excitement created a flutter through their hearts. They eagerly embraced the exhilarating rush of adrenaline through their veins. Shilpa and Surabhi loved scuba diving, and went deep into the sea to meet the sea turtles, jelly fish, and reefs. Ruby and Sona were interested in snorkelling.

Somu preferred to go for the lighthouse. He would be doing night diving in Havelock that offered the experience of hard and soft corals, humpback Parrot fish, Lionfish, Lobsters and Octopus.

When they had been busy exploring the excellent extravaganza of sea life, Riya and Rajan were pretty cool exchanging their feelings for treasured moments. Riya had opened up slowly, shared many things that were like riddles for Rajan and he was unable to solve them.

Riya missed her Papa a lot. He was like a precious possession to her. She reminisced the lovely park where he took her every evening. Life had the rosy hue that revealed a future stored with multicoloured opportunities for her, but everything went wrong on the day, the very day when the black Pazero hit her life.

Riya and her Papa, Mridul were coming back home. Their house was located in the suburbs and in a lonely area. It was seven o' clock in the evening when they were about to reach home. A black coloured Pazero came speedily from the other side of the road and stopped near them. There were three people along with the driver. One of them showed Mridul a piece of paper and enquired about the address written on it. When Mridul was going through it, the other two pressed Riya's nose with a handkerchief and she was ushered into the car. The man who had been talking to her Papa aimed his pistol towards his head, stepped into the car and the driver sped off.

Riya was eight years old at that time. She was completely shocked. When she came to her senses, she found herself sitting with ten other girls who were of same age. All of them were strapped to chairs. Their mouths were tied with a strip of cloth. A man with a beard was standing in front of them obeying the instructions given to him through his mobile phone.

"You must not raise your voice. I'm opening your mouth. Whatever I'm going to tell you, you have to do that." said the bearded man to Riya.

Riya shuddered. The man held the mobile in his hand and talked to somebody.

Then he turned and said "What's your Papa's phone number?"

Riya cried.

"Don't do all this drama. Tell me the number, else I am going to kill you."He aimed his pistol towards her.

"07xxxxxxxx6"replied Riya in a broken voice.

"Call him now and tell him that you are safe here with your uncle. The uncle is shooting a film and he needs you. He would send you back after a few days. Your father must not inform the police or anyone else. If he does anything of this kind, he would repent for that."

Riya burst out. Tears could not be controlled. An icy grip of fear rendered her speechless and trembling. She sobbed inconsolably, her body racked with unknown terror.

Anyhow she dialled her Papa and managed to repeat the dialogue.Then the phone was disconnected.

Riya once more took refuge to silence. Tears welled up in her eyes. Rajan patted her back showing his concern. Suddenly Riya split from his company, ran away and stared at him like a mad dog.

"You cheat! Bastard! Trying to seduce me? I hate you! I hate you! I hate you!….."

She started trembling. Like an angry bear she growled and fell unconscious after that.

Rajan was all in a fix. Crowd gathered and Riya was carried to the nearest lodge. The doctor was called. He pushed an injection. Slowly and slowly Riya came to her senses. Surabhi,Ruby and children arrived, but Somu was late. Ruby was shocked after listening to everything that happened. She apologized for Riya's behaviour. Riya dozed off once again. She was still under the influence of the medicine. An ambulance was called and they took her to the emergency ward in the nearby hospital.

Ruby narrated the incidents as told by Riya to Rajan and Surabhi once more. She also added the aftermath. Riya was imprisoned for a week. They stripped her at gunpoint and shot pictures as ordered by their leader. Ruby and Mridul could not make out how they got in such a pickle. They could not inform the police. The kidnappers could hurt the child or even kill her. Everyday their daughter talked to them that it was only a matter of fewer days. They must not worry as she was hale and hearty. She had to tell all this as they threatened to kill her. About a week passed by and there was a phone call. Rajan was asked to come near a government school that was situated near the Hooghly river next morning at four a.m. They told him not to disclose it to police or anyone else. Ruby and Mridul were completely shattered, but nothing could be done if they wished to get their daughter alive. They had to tell so many lies about Riya that could not be counted.

"Where is Riya ?Why is she not seen around? Did she run away from the house? Won't she miss her school?"

Innumerable questions were raised by the known and unknown people.

Riya came back, but she was under trauma. She had been raped by two of the gangsters before she was handed over to her parents. They neither killed her nor did they sell her to the community that was involved in trafficking.

It was a vendetta planned by one of Mridul's friend. Mridul was helpless. He himself was involved in this kind of thing. Ruby did not know anything about it. Later Mridul could not hold himself back and explained everything. Ruby did not utter a single word. She was numb with grief How could Mridul do such things? What made him so greedy that led his own daughter to suffer so much? Could he ever think of the other children he had helped in trafficking?

How much they and their parents had suffered!

Ruby could never forgive him. Not in this life. She narrated everything to Surabhi and broke down. Surabhi tried to console her, but she was scared. It could happen with Shilpa or Sona. She felt she was stuck in a quagmire. Was Rajan hiding anything from her? Did he also hurt Riya? No it couldn't be. She felt like a drowning child who tried to hold the straw floating in the water. He could never be a part of such heinous crime. But who knows? Human mind is like an ocean. The depth can't be fathomed.

"Why was Riya so upset? What did you do to her?"Surabhi inquired after coming back to their hotel.

"Are you nuts? A maniac——am I? How could you utter such words? When Riya started crying, I just patted her back and tried to console her. That's all what happened and she shot like a boomerang. Isn't she a psycho?"Rajan retorted.

Surabhi felt ashamed,but Ruby's words haunted her mind. They lay on their bed without facing each other. Riya had created a borderline between them. Their pleasure-trip was spoiled. Shilpa guessed something, but Sona did not know anything about Riya. However they felt low after Riya fell ill.

Next morning they had to visit Cellular Jail.

"What would be the fate of Mridul if his crime is detected.," Surabhi thought.

"Would he be sent to Cellular jail? Oops! What a stupid lady I am! How could he be sent there? This prison was used for the political prisoners during British reign. The freedom fighters were sent there by the British government. Now it has become a tourist attraction as it is a national monument."So Mridul's coming to Cellular Jail was out of question.

After the complementary breakfast they got ready for the trip, but before they left they had to find out how Riya was. They moved towards the hospital. Riya had come back to her senses. She was weak. She was not eating anything. The doctor advised her to take rest. She missed her Papa, but Ruby didn't agree to send for him. They were staying separately. She did not inform the police about his misdeeds because it could have affected their daughter. Riya was ignorant about her Papa's involvement with the criminals. Ruby could not hurt her feelings. So she tried to pacify her.

"Papa is busy,my darling! Please don't get swayed away by your whims. Eat something and be strong to fight the odds and meet challenges. You have to be a fighter dear,come on."Ruby tried to cheer up her daughter. Surabhi and Shilpa caressed Riya and left for their destination and promised to meet her later.

Riya was released from the hospital next day. Ruby and Somu decided to go back to Kolkata. They had fixed an appointment with a psychiatrist. Riya should get better treatment,they thought.

Surabhi and her children went to witness the Jarawa tribe with the guide. Rajan stayed at the hotel as he was not feeling well.

Jarawa were very hostile and were completely naked. They were at the primitive stage of the civilization. The guide who took them to several spots narrated their journey of vengeance. They never accepted the intruders. The government tried its level best to make them civilized. They thought that the civilized people would kill them. The guide also informed them about North Sentinel island. Shilpa insisted on visiting that place, but it was strictly forbidden for the visitors. Two fishermen had tried to fish illegally near the island. They were shot dead by the sentinel archers. Government had strived hard to make friends with them, but it was of no avail. So their tour ended with the visit to Dugong creek. They met the Ong population who were quite friendly. They accepted the food, clothes and medicines provided by the government. Surabhi bought a piece of handicraft made by them. They also could make canoes. A primary school was there for their education. However, many of them had become alcoholic that had taken toll on their lives.

The tour package of Surabhi and Rajan was going to end, leaving a seamless and unforgettable experience. With the indelible imprints on the memories, they packed and headed for Kolkata. Shilpa and Sona felt morose as their vacation had ended. Once more they had to join the dullsville life.

Rajan was very upset and could not enjoy the last part of the trip. He started avoiding his wife and children. Surabhi was also ashamed of being over sensitive. A strained relationship between them caused to give rise to many unwanted issues they could never think of.They reached Kolkata. Rajan had to join his office next day. He was diabetic.

Surabhi was quite strict about his diet. Every morning he would ask for his tea and would coax Surabhi to give him one spoon of sugar at least, but hardly he would be able to convince her. It was like a hide and seek game. In the evening when he came back home, he would bribe Sona with chocolates and chips, ask him to open the fridge and find out if he could locate the box of sweets gifted by Ranga Masi. Surabhi would find it out and shout at him and the little boy.

"What's up? Both father and son are trying to snatch away my peace. Who would be responsible if he falls sick? Listen Rajan, already you are going through a hectic schedule and so much stress. Why don't you take care of youself? You are a sugar-patient. If you take so many sweets at a time, your kidneys are going to fail. Already your heart is implanted with a stent. Please listen to me and follow the doctor's advice. And Sona I'm going to be rude, if you offer sweets to your Papa."

After coming back from Andaman, the scenario had changed. Rajan was completely deaf and dumb. He did everything, but would not talk to his wife and children. Surabhi left no stone unturned. She offered him sweets, coaxed him, caressed him like a child, but everything fell flat. Shilpa and Sona were unable to cheer him up with their antics, but who cared?

A month passed by. It was a weekend. The clock struck eight in the morning. Surabhi woke up late. She had a sleepless night crumbling in the bed. She cried, tried her best to creep in her husband's arms. Rajan did not respond. He was sleeping like a log. She fell asleep in the early morning. When she opened her eyes, Rajan was not there.

"Don't know how I can manage him. Why did I tell him all those words? Oh God! Please help me." Surabhi repented.

The morning sun gradually cast its vibrant warmth of noon, shadows shortened. Activities buzzed with heightened intensity, but Rajan couldn't be seen in the vicinity of their house. Surabhi called all her friends, but they knew nothing about him. She informed the local police station, but nothing came into being. Surabhi couldn't manage her school. She had to take sick leave. Her mother came to look after her and the children.

Time passed by, but nothing improved. Surabhi was suffering from depression and Rajan was nowhere to be seen. Surabhi's mom was restless. How long she had to stay with her she didn't know. One day she opened up,

"Su, please gather yourself. Please think about your children. Shilpa is growing up and Sona is still a kid. How long can I stay here leaving your Baba ?I have to take care of him too. He is a heart-patient. I have to be vigilant about him. Now join your school. Now it's you who has to share all the responsibility. Please let me go now."Her mother said.

Surabhi pondered on her words. She thought she couldn't lose her Baba. She regained her confidence and joined her school.

The wheels of time rolled on and on. No trace of Rajan could be found anywhere. However, after six months he could be located in Bashirhaat where he had got himself transferred from his office. His main motto was to find out the culprits behind Child trafficking. Surabhi met him and coaxed him to stay with them, to leave all those weird ideas and lead the life of an ordinary person peacefully. Rajan refused.

"Let me do some good work for these helpless children, else our country would be ruined. Pleae don't cry. It would be better for you and the children to stay away from me. The criminals can be dangerous for you all. Please don't let anyone know about my mission. I am always there with you and my children. I would send a large amount to your bank account in the name of your father every month, so don't worry." said Rajan. Surabhi stared at him blankly and had to leave.

After a year, the water of the river Ichamati looked bloody. People had gathered near the bank of the river. Police came and recovered Rajan's body with bullet stains.

Chapter-5

"Ladies and gentlemen! Thank you for choosing Indigo. We're going to land on Veer Savarkar Airport. Please fasten your seat belts." The announcement brought Shilpa back from Bashirhaat to the present scenario.

Aruni, the sub-inspector, collected their briefcases from the overhead cupboard and both came out of the aircraft. Confidently, Shilpa moved towards the exit gate. Her sharp observant eyes were vigilantly scanning everything. She was received by the Portblair police. They sat in the jeep with a few armed cops and reached the guesthouse.

Within half an hour Shilpa became ready for the adrenaline-fuelled pursuit. Every moment counted. She gave a few instructions to Aruni who had already set her sights on the mission. Next Shilpa started her expedition. Portblair police were ready for it. With a strategic planning and the armed force, Shilpa headed for the destination. The informer had been faster to send her the location this time. Shilpa was hoping against hope. This time she might be successful.

The man was staying in a hotel that was a marvel of modern engineering and luxury. Nestled beneath the crystalline waters of the Andaman sea, the hotel catered to the rhythmic ebb and flow of the ocean that lulled the guests into a strange world where the sunlight illuminated the elegant design and décor. The expansive windows of the suites depicted the mesmerizing panorama of vibrant marine life transporting the guests to a surreal world of tranquillity and wonder. It offered gourmet dining experiences and immersive underwater entertainment, a unique fusion of opulence and adventure.

He had never sensed that Shilpa would chase her in that aquatic sanctuary.

How could a woman be so obsessed with criminals? How could she be so strong and hardy? However, he laughed like a blood thirsty maniac who didn't know anything other than money, yet à tinge of fear lurked somewhere in his mind. He had a physique that was honed through years of physical training.His steely gaze and confident swagger had a ruthless determination to achieve his goals. His calculating mind was capable of devising elaborate schemes. Like a force to be reckoned with and an enigma to be feared, he reigned supreme in his world of crime,but he had a gut feeling that something was going to happen that could cause a disastrous effect on his hard-earned wealth and dignity as the emperor of the underworld.

Shilpa and her team orchestrated a meticulous operation to reach Emerald Elsium. She was fully aware of the unique challenges posed by its underwater location. Utilizing specialized equipment and expertise in maritime navigation, she asked her crew to remain vigilant, scanning the horizon for any sign of the elusive criminal. She was ready to confront any type of obstacle lying in the path of their relentless pursuit of justice. Their vessel was slowly gliding across the surface of the sea when the sound of a helicopter hovering over their ship superseded the sound of the waves. Shilpa thought it could be a critical move by the culprit.

"Ma'am, look it has changed its direction. What does it mean?"

"Yes Ma'am! It seems to mislead us." said one of the cops from the local police.

Surrounded by the eerie silence of the sea,a voice resounded that Shilpa only could hear…

"Shilu! Follow the helicopter. You are about to reach your goal."It was her father's voice.

She ordered the crew to change the route and follow the chopper. With the rhythmic thump of the rotor blades cutting through the air, the helicopter headed towards north where the flickering lights disclosed the existence of a few small boats. Serving as a beacon of vigilance, the chopper scanned the turbulent waters below. The vessel with Shilpa and her team manoeuvred through the choppy waves. Their unwavering determination could hardly miss any sign of the fleeing suspect. The chase, amidst the vastness of the sea, had a crucial advantage with the helicopter's aerial perspective. It could be helpful in determining the fugitive's movements and directing the pursuit with precision. Each passing moment had been instrumental in highlighting the relentless pursuit of justice and the tension mounted amidst the unforgiving vastness of the ocean. Their vessel had been close to the boats. With each cresting wave and gust of wind, the chase intensified. Though the fugitive's options dwindled,his resolve remained unyielding, determined to evade capture at any cost.

The flickering lights of the boats could be seen far away gliding across the sea, and then a sudden pounding surf ….!

"Fast..move faster !We can't miss him …"Shilpa's voice got suppressed by the ambient noise of the wind and the sea.

They charted a course through the pristine waters towards the sound. The supersonic bullets pierced through the air, creating sonic boom. The sound of the explosion was not a cacophony of different sounds, rather it was from both directions. The sound was like one blast per pull of a trigger. Then smoke filled the air.

Skrrrah…..pap-pap—dut—dut du-du—dun—dun and the sound of the sea accompanying the fluttering sound of the sea animals were cinematic. A few cops had dived into the sea and they luckily caught hold of the man's legs and could drag him towards their boat. The helicopter's aerial perspective provided a great opportunity to implement their strategies. The man struggled, but his drunkenness prevented him from making any attempt to move. He was completely unconscious. The force pulled him on the boat. Draped in a funky black leather vest he was lying like a log, hard hit by decades of struggle and suffering. His face was framed by a rugged beard,serving as a cloak of anonymity and veiling his identity, but amplifying the aura of mystery and danger. Beneath the each scar etched into the weathered skin,a glimmer of cunning intelligence was there that hinted at the calculating mind.As he was not in his senses,his eyes were closed, yet his features revealed a spark of ruthless determination. Shilpa heaved a sigh of relief as the man was now at least unable to outsmart even the most vigilant adversary. The doctor in the police force examined him and pushed an injection. The man opened his eyes slowly,but again fell asleep. Shilpa and her team hurried to the shore so that the man could get a better treatment.Their boat reached the shore after thirty minutes. It was midnight. They all got down. An ambulance was already there and the man was handed over to the local police officials.

However, Shilpa and Aruni were always with them. When Shilpa looked at the face of the man keenly, she had a faint picture of someone who had a lot of similarities with this fellow. Suddenly the name Mridul, Riya's father, flashed in her mind and she just couldn't believe her eyes.

"OMG! How Riya would react if she comes to know about her father!"

Yes, how could she forget the girl whom she had met in Andaman in her childhood! And it was due to this girl only her Papa left them forever. However Riya received cognitive behavioural therapy and after six months she could finally live a better life. She was bright in her studies and qualified for I.E.S. and got a government job. She stayed with her mother who had retired as a bank manager. They were not at all concerned about Mridul and lived a carefree life.

Shilpa and Aruni came back to their headquarters with the culprit who survived, but had lost his memory. The case was dismissed and he was sent to an asylum. He was very calm and relaxed, sitting in the corner of the room. Shilpa went to meet him, and wished to ask many questions about his family, but he didn't reply a word, only stared like a vanquished hero.

Chapter-6

Shilpa's mother had retired from her job. She stayed with her son. Sona had become an engineer and was settled in U.S.A. He had two cute kids and a beautiful wife who loved her husband and his family very much.

Shilpa didn't marry even if many of her classmates had proposed her. Her mother was very upset. She wondered if at all she would marry, but Shilpa wished to achieve her goals that could not be fulfilled by her father.

That day she was suddenly feeling very relaxed, but was missing her Papa.

"Papa! Where are you? Look I have been able to fulfil your dreams. Won't you come and give me a hug?"

Dusk descended like a gentle veil. The sky like a canvas, painted with strokes of pink, orange and indigo blended seamlessly across the horizon. The day surrendered to night. Shadows lengthened. A quiet hush fell over the world. The occasional rustle of the leaves and the distant chirping of the crickets broke the silence. In this transition of day and night, the world seemed to hold its breath suspended in a peaceful embrace before darkness enveloped all.

Shilpa looked at the pole star where she could find her Papa's countenance with a bright smile.

"Papa I made it! My dream came true! Bless me Papa."

"Yes my darling! Never give up." She could hear a faint voice. She put her cup down on the side table and folded her hands in prayer.

Chapter-7

Mridul was involved in a number of cases like fake drug trafficking in which Triparna got involved. It was Shilpa who rescued her from that. She became one of their close friends and Triparna didn't even just love her but adored her. She was like a family member and was invited on any occasion. Soham also guided her like a big brother in her moves. She had come to know many things about the terrorists. They were like an oasis in her dry and dreary life that always seemed overcrowded with the endless crimes, but she was rewarded for her efforts and was transferred to Delhi as Deputy Superintendent of Police. This came as a blow to Triparna's life. However, they were in touch with her.

Triparna was growing up and was very curious about the complexities of human mind. She had shared everything with Shilpa, even the Goa incident.

Actually, it happened one year ago when Shilpa was not known to them.

It was her mom's birthday. Triparna was busy in the kitchen. Her mom had played forty five years of her innings safely, but Triparna? She had only stepped into the nineteenth year that was filled with a platter of different types of experiences making her brave and bold, but what about preparing meal in the kitchen ?It was a far-fetched story for her. She just imagined the scene in the college next day when out of the blue she would announce,

"Hey guys! I have been able to win my mom's heart. Just guess how? It's true darlings. She had loved the roasted chicken prepared by me."

Triparna's friends would never change their tunes, she thought. They could never imagine her holding a spatula, stirring vegetables in the kitchen. They, at least, did know that Sumana, her mom, could transcend mere recipes into delightful culinary experiences. With a creative flair she could transform simple ingredients into gastronomic masterpieces, making the kitchen a realm of beautiful imaginations where the complexities of flavour and cooking methods elevated every meal to an unforgettable feast for the taste buds and left the diners crave more, but Triparna….!No way. For her friends, Triparna with her specs on her nose, would always be surfing the Google, finding some clues that might be helpful for Criminal psychology and jotting down the details about the minds behind the crimes.

She washed the chicken and marinated it with lemon juice and spices as she knew her mother would relish the roasted chicken with boiled vegetables. Infusing each dish with flavours reminiscent of cherished memories, she could hardly forget how her Papa reacted once after coming home from work. She was six years old at that time. He opened the lock, came in and took her in his arms and peeped into the kitchen.

"Wow! What a beautiful aroma! Dear princess! How are you today? Your mom is a magician. She can make the flavours, dance harmoniously and the textures, tantalize the taste buds. Now just wait and we are going to taste today's marvellous dish."

"No Papa! Don't! Mamma would be very angry."

"Who cares dear? I am your Papa, and your Papa can do anything. He can tame a lion. He can bring a pearl for his princess from the ocean. Never be afraid of anything. Always stay on the path of honesty and integrity and climb the ladder of success. Now listen to me. Stand here quietly. By the way where's your mom?"

"She is taking shower. Today Priya aunty, her friend is going to visit us."

"We would finish before she finds us out."

He then opened the lid of the casserole, took out a big leg-piece, kept it in a bowl and gave it to her.

"Hold it carefully and enjoy. I will take this piece."

He took another bowl and took out one from the vessel.

Both started their tasting sessions and the climax reached when her mom stood with a stick in her hand and glared at them.

"I thought it must be the pussycat in our neighbourhood. I wished to scare it with this stick. Now what can be the punishment for these big cats?" her mom retorted.

"Oh! No! We also wished to scare her away, but she offered us, and we were enchanted by the smell of the beautiful chicken curry. Please forgive Miss, only for this time." Papa said folding his hands, and then held his ears. It was ridiculous to find Soham Das, the famous drug inspector who was six feet tall and a handsome young man in his forties, doing such antics.

Then all three burst out laughing and the noisy buzzing of the phone forced them to restrain themselves from enjoying the simple pleasures of life.

"Hello! Who is speaking? Can't hear. Ok....! Where is he? Wagah border?

Ok...Coming in a minute. Ask the force to join me on the highway."

And her Papa left home hurriedly. Mom coaxed him to have his dinner, but he didn't lose a single moment and started his jeep. He only had told her that a gang of criminals were coming through Wagah border, and he had to arrest them. However, he warned her not to disclose this to anyone. He kissed her and Triparna on her forehead and left.

Triparna and her mom bid him goodbye without knowing that this would be his fatal departure from his home. Triparna felt low and her mom tried to cheer her up.

"Let Papa come home, and we all would go to watch the brilliant show held in the Wagah border.", her mother tried to please her.

"Where is it mom? What is the brilliant thing?" Triparna inquired.

"Well Tiru dear! Let me show you something and she came with a map.

"Look, this is the Indo -Pak border. India is our country and Pakistan is our neighbouring country. The Change of guard within handshaking distances makes a charming spectacle. The pomp and pageantry of Beating the Retreat-steals the show. Beating the Retreat is very popular as the soldiers from both countries march in perfect harmony, going through the steps of bringing down their respective national flags. The sun goes down. The nationalistic fervour rises. Lights are switched on marking the end of the day and the thunderous applause echoes everywhere." Sumona said.

"Ok …" Triparna said.

In the meantime, Priya aunty dropped in, and they enjoyed the meal. Triparna missed her Papa very much and absentmindedly she unpacked one of her boxes that her Papa had gifted on her last birthday. The box contained a small ring with a red ruby. "Wear this ring whenever you want to meet me, and I would come." Papa had said. She recalled and wore that ring. Priya aunty with her pet, a beautiful Pomeranian was about to leave when the phone rang.

"Hello Ma'am! Please come to the police station. We are sending the jeep. It's urgent." This was a call from the local police station. An officer had called.

Triparna found her mom completely perturbed. What happened? Is Soham safe? She was barraged with numerous questions by Triparna, but the answers were not clear enough to remove her doubts. The gurgling sound of the engine broke their reverie and Sumana, Triparna and Priya had stepped into the jeep. Sumana had asked Triparna to stay behind with Priya auntie, but she insisted and accompanied her. The officer said Soham had met with a fatal accident and was carried to a nearby hospital. It was a terrorist attack. The terrorists triggered a bullet and Soham fell on his knees. He tried hard to get hold of the pistol lying nearby, but one of the attackers managed to hit his head and Soham became unconscious. They escaped despite the chase. However, Sumana had to be strong and meet the challenge.

Sumana and Triparna burst into tears. However, Priya consoled them anyhow and advised them to be brave. The jeep reached the hospital. The officer asked them to wait until the surgery was done. Triparna was numb with grief. She was only praying to God.

"O God please, please let my Papa live. Papa says that those who are honest and do good deeds, you are very kind to them. Then why did you hurt Papa? Dear God, why are you being so mean?" she was talking to her own self.

Sumana looked pale.

"If anything goes wrong, what will happen to us?" she thought.

Priya was trying to make things better for them, but all her efforts were futile. Triparna was busy with her prayers and Sumana stared blankly at the operation theatre where Soham was fighting with life and death.

It was about midnight when the doctor came out from the O.T. Sumana rushed towards him. Priya followed her. The officer from the police department was also present. They were all eager to listen to the verdict to be announced by the doctor accompanied by a junior doctor.

The doctor looked at the faces and spoke, "We can't say anything now. After twenty-four hours, we would be able to see the consequences. It's a bit serious. Unless he comes to his senses, we don't know what is going to happen."

Sumana asked, "Can we get a glimpse of him? May I go inside and touch him?"

"No Ma'am. Please wait and watch. He can get infections. So, we have to be careful. Pray to God that everything will be alright. Please be strong and take care of your child." the junior doctor said and followed the surgeon.

Sumana didn't know what to do. Priya tried to convince her, but she was like a rock not responding to anything. Her mind became a battleground, tangled in a labyrinth of fears and doubts. Apprehensions danced on the fringes of consciousness, weaving a tapestry of anxiety stretching infinitely into the darkness. As night enveloped the hospital corridor, the apprehensions whispered secrets. Every creak of the floorboards and rustle of the wind outside seemed to magnify the sense of unease. She accepted the submission to fate; nothing was in her hand.

Triparna, however, did not cease praying. She had closed her eyes and was chanting mantras that she learnt from her granny, long ago. She believed in her Papa's saying, "If you are righteous and love your fellow beings, God will always be there for you."

It was five o'clock. The first light of dawn broke through the horizon, as if a beacon of hope pierced through the darkness of night. The world woke up to embrace a new day, full of promises and positive vibes. The gentle hues of pink and gold painted the sky. It cast a warm glow upon the earth. The warmth of life thrived again with the crying of the newborns. It was a fresh start for a beautiful and better tomorrow.

The junior doctors were on rounds. Sumana and Priya rushed to one of them and inquired about Soham. He said that Soham was still unconscious, it was not unusual, and they should not lose hope. Priya left as she had to inform her boss and would have to take leave from her office so that Sumana could feel a bit comfortable. She was single and lived with her mother whom she had already informed about Sumana's predicament. She wanted to convince Triparna that she should go with her and have some breakfast and again could come back with her. Triparna was adamant. She would not leave the place until she met her Papa. However, the officers were there and Sumana requested Priya to leave as she was stable and would look after her daughter.

Two hours passed and it was eight o'clock in the morning when the surgeon who operated, came. He went inside the cabin where Soham lay unconscious. Two junior doctors and nurses accompanied him. Sumana and Triparna were all agog to know the results. After a few minutes the door creaked and one of the nurses called Sumana and declared that Soham had come back to his senses. He was out of danger. His left leg where the bullet hit had to be amputated, and he might suffer from paralysis for several years in his left side. Sumana felt devastated, yet heaved a sigh of relief. At least he was alive! Triparna could not comprehend many things but was happy to hear that her papa was alive. After some time, they were allowed to meet Soham one by one. Soham was unable to talk. He only made gestures and smiled faintly.

"Don't worry Papa! You would be alright in a few days. I am praying to *Bajrangbali* every time. He would help you to get well soon.", Triparna shook hands with her Papa.

Sumana tried to hide her tears with a fake smile. Priya also said many good things to cheer him up.

"Hello Soham! We all are going to throw a big party when you are back home. Cheer up dear. It's a matter of only a few days." Priya said.

But all of them knew that life won't be the same again for him. Later in the evening his colleagues dropped in. Some of them were really worried to find him in that situation, but a few were also happy that they would get their promotion. It was a matter of concern that he would lose his job as he had only one leg and would not be able to enjoy the inexhaustible physical agility he had.

After a month he was released from the hospital. Sumana had to find a job as Soham was offered voluntary retirement and he had to accept. This caused a lot of depression to him. He was confined to his wheelchair most of the time and needed help from the nurse for doing anything. He could not move his left part of the body freely and his speech also was indistinct. He slurred his words while talking and this made him feel uneasy. He was cross with Sumana, would throw anything in his reach to hurt her, wanted to shout at her but couldn't. Then tears trickled down from his eyes that he wished to hide. Sumana tried to please and coax him, but all went in vain.

Sumana cried a lot. "Dear God! Please help me out. I am so tired of all these. How can I get back my evergreen Soham who would jump and lift his daughter up in his arms. When would he be normal again? Please let me have the patience to bear all this."

Only Triparna could make him happy. After coming back from school, she sat near her Papa and would read the newspaper for him. She would open the laptop and then would ask him to use his right hand to write the mails. She would talk to him vigorously and encourage him to answer so that his tongue could move freely.

Sumana and Triparna had to take a test of their patience and Soham started to improve. His speech became clearer. His strong willpower, and Triparna's patience and determination let him win the challenges. He would now talk to his close friends and would ask about the terrorists he wanted to arrest. His juniors would get advice from him about any complicated case and act accordingly. If they were able to arrest them, they would come with a box of sweets and would say,

"Sir! It's only because of your suggestions we have been able to win." and Soham felt happy.

Triparna was growing up into a fine young lady. She passed her Senior secondary examination with flying colours. Then she opted for Criminal psychology instead of choosing the normal courses like Medicine, Engineering or Administrative services. Everyone thought that she would follow the footsteps of her father, but she chose a completely different genre to build her career. She had seen her Papa following the path of honesty, justice and sincerity. She always wanted to know how or what provokes the human minds to commit such crimes that her Papa tried to get rid of. She could not find answers to many questions and discussed them with Soham.

After a few years Soham was able to walk with his crutch. Every day in the evening he would go out and sit in the park, but Triparna would always be there by his side. Triparna would depict the incidents she witnessed or heard about fraud, forgery, terrorism, child abuse and many serious topics about human mind. Her Papa would tell her that human mind is like an ocean.

"Papa, how would you define trauma?"

"Tiru, there are high tides and low tides in the ocean. Traumas are like high tides. During high tides, the ocean swells to its highest levels, enveloping shorelines and reclaiming sandy beaches with its ruthless advance. Sea water surges with powerful vitality, but during low tides the sea is calm and quiet with the water flowing smoothly. In the same way, human mind is full of complications during trauma that encompasses a range of distressing events and myriads of complex emotions like fear and anxiety, shattering the smooth flow of life.

"In today's fast paced world, people often fall prey to the temptation of cutting corners and restoring to unethical means to move forward. The lure of instant access and the promise of achieving everything quickly like the instant noodles have become the norm. For this relentless pursuit of efficiency and convenience, the insidious grip of corruption blurs the lines between right and wrong. People who prioritize selfish interests over integrity discard the moral compasses. Greed tightens its hold on them. Corruption spreads its dark tendrils through all the spheres of life, shading its shadows over trust and security giving birth to cynicism and keeping alive injustice. The dire consequences of prioritizing expediency and material gain would lead to decaying ethical values and the welfare of the society." he would add.

Triparna's Papa wrote many books on the strategy of eradicating corruption. He then opened a coaching center for those who wished to qualify in the exams held for UPSC and Triparna grew up into a bright confident girl dreaming high to soar in the sky.

Her mom had a lot of expectations from her as she was their only child. She never prevented Triparna from doing anything she wanted. The bonding was eternal. The trust could not be shattered. She believed that children must be confident, and they should be allowed to enjoy their freedom. She did not believe in the gender discrimination. She had allowed her daughter to learn karate. Triparna wished to learn horse riding and she never said "No" to anything. Soham also encouraged her to learn more and more. It could be swimming or painting, singing or dancing. Triparna too, could never betray them.

All three of them celebrated Sumana's birthday with pomp and show. A few of their close friends also joined them. Sumana relished the chicken and the delicious cup cakes made by Triparna.

"OMG! My cute princess has now grown up into a royal Chef. It was a meal to tempt even the jaded palate. I am proud of you, darling!" Sumana declared.

"Whose daughter, is she? She is just like her Papa, isn't she? Hasn't our little angel grown up into a gorgeous queen with beauty and brains?" exclaimed Sohan.

Triparna was then doing her third semester. They had a long vacation tagged with the weekend. Her close friends like Sophia, Amaya and Olivia were adventurous and wished to utilize their vacation.

"Let's visit Deegha or Mandarmoni and enjoy our holidays. I hope all of us would be able to get permission from our parents." Olivia suggested.

"No dear! I have visited these places several times with my family. I am not interested to go there." Amaya retorted.

"Hey guys! Why not Goa? It would be thrilling enough to visit the seashore and taste the Goan food! Moreover, I have one of my cousins who can arrange everything for us, and we would visit the Casino for extraordinary Gaming experience. What's your idea?" Sophia was full of excitement.

"Cheers to that!" Triparna, Olivia and Amaya shouted.

They were so excited that they started counting the days. An itinerary was planned after consulting with Sophia's cousin Loyola, who, however, declared that she would not be there to attend them as she had to go on a tour for some office work. They could enjoy her house free of cost and the key would be kept with the landlord who was a very nice fellow and stayed upstairs.

Triparna explained everything to her parents. She told them about their plan to visit the casino quite frankly and honestly. Sumana got a little apprehensive when she heard about that but didn't object. She trusted her daughter and knew that she would never indulge in anything wrong.

Soham gave her many pieces of advice.

"Goa is a place to enjoy. You can visit the iconic beaches of Calangute and Baga. Palolem and Agonda are the tranquil shores. Its coastline boasts a wealth of stunning vistas and water sports activities. You can immerse yourselves in the region's colonial heritage by exploring the historic churches and quaint Portuguese villages."

"Oh! Yes! You must not miss the culinary flavours that are equally enticing. The fusion of Indian, Portuguese and international cuisines would tantalize your taste buds at every turn." he added.

"Yes Papa! It will be all fun. I am going to post pictures every day. No worries, Papa."

One fine morning Triparna with her friends boarded their flight from Netaji Subhas Chandra Bose International airport.

All of them reached on time except Olivia. Triparna, Amaya and Sophia were calling her one by one, but her phone was switched off. All three of them felt very low as they were being asked to go for security checks.

"What happened to Olivia? Why is she not answering?" Sophia said.

"Don't panic. She would reach! Might be stuck in the traffic. It's a long way from Kalikapur." announced Triparna.

"If she doesn't reach, it would be a disaster. She should start quite early as she knows well how the traffic is. She is so irresponsible!" Sophia was really annoyed.

Tension thickened as the clock ticked past eleven a.m! Only ten minutes left for the closure of the counter for boarding pass. The eager anticipation for a beautiful experience simmered with uncertainty and frustration. Each passing moment strained the bounds of patience. Three of them then exchanged glances that betrayed a mounting sense of unease pondering on the reasons for Olivia's delay. Amidst whispered comments and anxious apprehensions, time seemed to crawl like a snail, amplifying the tension.

"Hey guys! Look she is there near the counter." Amaya screamed like a child, forgetting everything.

Smiles illuminated the faces of Triparna, Sophia and Amaya. Excitement surged through like a palpable wave, marking the end of the anxious wait and beginning of renewed camaraderie. Laughter and conversation filled the air with embraces and hugs. Time seemed to stand still, reminding them of the special bond shared among them and the priceless value of cherished companionship that was reaffirmed.

"Oli! It's too much for us." burst Triparna.

"Really, we hated you!" said Sophia.

"But bro! Just tell us what held you back so long?" asked Amaya.

Their security check had been done and they were waiting to board, chattering constantly.

"Dear guys! Please forgive me. My alarm clock went off. My phone was not charged, and I didn't have time to search for the charger. Yesterday my mom had a bad headache and fell unconscious. We had to spend a lot of time in the hospital. They did an MRI, pushed one injection, then she was able to walk. However, today she is perfectly healthy. I thought I would cancel my trip, but Papa told me not to worry. He would take care of her. I should rush, else would miss the flight, but you see I am not as excited as I had been until I know the report of the MRI." Olivia narrated her story.

"So sorry dear! Everything would be better. Don't worry." said Triparna.

"Extremely sorry dear! All would be well." said Sophia.

"Cheer up baby! Nothing can be wrong as we have never done anything wrong." exclaimed Amaya.

The passengers started moving and with the group now complete, they crackled with excitement, infused with a sense of anticipation for the adventures lying ahead. They took selfies and then occupied their seats.

Time passed by in the blink of an eye. They watched movies, munched snacks and coke to their hearts' content. The captain announced that they were going to land in Dabolim airport within ten minutes. They must tie their seatbelts and be safe. After a few minutes, the plane landed at the airport. Then they boarded down and a bus was waiting for them to take them to the airport. They availed and were safe. All four of them called their parents and told them that they landed safely and were about to leave the airport after collecting their baggage.

Sophia also connected with Loyola, her cousin. She told her that her car with a driver was waiting for them, and they must not hire a taxi. They could use her car as long as they wished. All felt very good. Even if they thought they could do everything right and on their own, they had butterflies in their stomachs as the place was completely unknown for them.

Triparna recalled her Papa's sermons, "Be careful with the guides. They are very tricky. They know how to exploit the tourists."

So, when they found the driver who belonged to Sophia's cousin, they depended on him thoroughly and got every suggestion from him.

They reached Loyola's home within an hour. Nestled along the picturesque coastline of Goa, the house offered a diverse array of attractions with its sun-kissed beaches. The driver gave them the keys and they entered a house that had all the modern amenities. The antique furniture posed a contrast keeping up the symmetry with the colonial heritage.

"At last," exclaimed Triparna.

"Finally...", all three of them screamed.

They opened the fridge and found some cooked recipes stored for them. All of them enjoyed the food and they were feeling more comfortable and confident. Olivia, however, was wondering whether her mom was alright. So, she called her Papa. Others also waited eagerly for the news from Olivia's Papa.

"Papa, how is Mom? What did the doctor say?" Olivia said.

"Don't worry beta, she is alright. It occurred due to her fasting as she stayed without food for a long time. Now she has learnt a lesson and is taking her food timely. You enjoy and take care of yourself."

"Moms are like that only, you know! She won't listen to us at all and will miss her breakfast most of the days." Olivia said.

"Really! You are perfectly right." retorted Amaya whose mom was an ardent follower of Saibaba.

"Now come on guys. Let's go for a walk on the beach, and tomorrow we will visit the other places." said Triparna.

"But where are we going to dine?" Sophia, who was the most foodie amongst them, reacted.

"Yes yes! Don't be late guys! Hurry up!" Triparna, like a matron, was trying to manage them. She was mature enough to govern them as she had seen life. The other three friends of hers were their Mommy's pet or Papa's pet. They were a bit childish and were impulsive. Triparna analyzed every situation logically and was never swayed away by emotion.

The seashore food stalls in Goa welcomed them with the tantalizing aroma of fresh seafood and spices. The colourful stalls offered a feast for the eyes as well as senses. The sound of crashing waves added to the sizzle of the grill. The menus consisted of succulent grilled fish and prawns to spicy Goan curries and crispy fritters.

"Ah what a beautiful aroma! Let's go with this one!" exclaimed Sophia.

"Ah wait! First find out the rate." Triparna declared.

"Oh Tiru! Why are you being like Papa? Please don't stop us from enjoying." said Amaya.

"Ok, but we must spend our money wisely. Let's go dear. Don't feel low." Triparna replied.

They chose to sit outside under a gorgeous umbrella, ordered grilled fish and Goan curry and rice, soaking in the sea breeze with panoramic views of the ocean.

After finishing the meal, they moved back inside the house that was nearby.

Then they watched a movie and fell asleep as they were done in by all the travel and the stress caused by Olivia's delay.

Next morning laughter and conversation filled the air as the eager planning of future adventures began. The driver came and took them to the historic landmarks like Basilica of Bom Jesus, Fort Aguada and Chapora Fort. They were charmed to see the Portuguese architecture. In the evening they embarked on a cruise. The vessel sailed along the azure waters of the Arabian Sea. The breathtaking views of the palm-fringed beaches, ancient forts and picturesque villages stole their hearts. Onboard a myriad of amenities and activities waited for them. They took part in the live music performances. Amaya was a very good singer and Olivia was a beautiful dancer. Both participated and Sophia and Triparna clapped together with the beat. They made videos so that they could post them on social media. Sophia was glued to the tables displaying delectable seafood buffets and was enjoying the sunset dinner. In the meantime, Triparna went on the deck to explore hidden coves and to enjoy the tranquillity of the open sea.

After spending two hours on the sea, they took selfies, came back to the shore and found the driver who was waiting for them. Then they headed for Loyola's house.

They had one more day before their vacation ended. So next day they went shopping. All four of them bought traditional Goan textiles with vibrant colours, intricate designs and skilled craftsmanship. The shirts they bought for their Papas reflected the region's unique blend of Indian and Portuguese influences. The Kunbi saris and Fugdi dresses adorned with traditional intricate embroidery while embracing contemporary styles were the other items that enriched their shopping bags. Triparna didn't buy many whereas Amaya, Sophia and Olivia had overloaded their bags. Triparna warned them that they would have to pay extra amount for their luggage, but they ignored.

Their final destination was the Casino where the thrill of gaming, luxury and entertainment stole the show. It offered an ambience of opulence and excitement. An atmosphere of sophistication with dazzling chandeliers, plush carpets and sleek furnishings created a sense of grandeur. Rows of slot machines and gaming tables buzzed with activity. Amaya, Sophia and Olivia started trying their luck at blackjack, roulette and poker amidst an ambience charged with anticipation. Triparna just watched her friends screaming and yelling. With live entertainment, elegant bars and restaurants serving up gourmet cuisine and handcrafted cocktails, all three of them got enchanted and acted like the lunatics. It was high time and next day they had their flights in the afternoon. They were giggling a lot. After a while Olivia started crying and shouted,

"Why all of you are staring at me? What have I done? Only tasted a pinch of marijuana! What's wrong in that? Don't scare me! How relaxed I feel! Just like a bird soaring in the sky!" Olivia continued in a strange voice.

Triparna was completely taken aback. From where they got marijuana was beyond her imagination.

When she asked them, they reacted and said, "Why it must be in your purse too. We all found it in our purses." What? She checked her new purse and found the same. She could match each and every action what she had learnt from her father. He had been a drug inspector. He used to talk about the drug dealers how they used to trap others in the business. They would drop the drug packets in someone else's bags and then the police would find him out and he would be behind the bars.

In the meantime, there was a loud uproar, and everyone started running here and there. Amidst the flashing lights and barks of commands, patrons were caught off guard as officers swarmed the gaming floors. With the cacophony of sirens and commotion, the tables were swiftly shut down and they seized the gambling equipment.

Triparna was dragging her three friends as she knew that the police would check their purses too, but all three of them were crazy cuckoos, they were revolting against Triparna and wished to stay there. The air crackled with tension and Triparna anyhow staggered and creaked along the exit door leaving them there. Like a thief she crawled towards their car and tried to locate the driver. The driver could not be seen anywhere. She took out the pouch of the drug and threw it down the lake stealthily. The area swarmed with the cops who were checking the cars, and the people around and the shops nearby. Triparna tried to connect with the driver, but the phone was switched off. She also called her friends, but all three mobiles were not responding.

"Oh my God! What will I do now!" she felt very bad.

Suddenly she found her friends tied with handcuffs, the police dragging them towards the van. She ran towards them and begged the police to let them go, but none listened to her as they had been caught with the drugs. Olivia, Amaya and Sophia were all in tears and begged her to do something for them. Triparna asked them to have patience and assured them that she was going to hire a lawyer for them. She called Loyola, but she didn't attend the call. Triparna did not lose her patience and tried again and again. After fifteen minutes she called back.

"Hello! Who is this?"

"Hello! Hello! I am Tiru, Sophia's friend. Did you forget me?"

"Oh no! Sorry dear! I couldn't recall the number. I had been too busy. Tomorrow I would be back. Hope all is fine with you. Please send the driver to the airport. I would be there at around eight a.m in the morning."

"Oh dear! We are really in trouble and the driver is nowhere to be seen. Your car is parked near the Golden Sands Casino. The key is with your driver. Sophie, Ama and Oli are in police custody. I would tell you everything as you come back. Your presence is absolutely essential. Please come back as soon as possible."

"Oh! No! What are you saying? I just can't believe. However, cancel your tickets as soon as possible, else a lot of money would be wasted. Don't worry, I would reach tomorrow morning and book a cab. Bye!"

"Ok. Bye!" Triparna felt a little bit better.

She booked a cab and headed towards home. She had a gut feeling about the smugglers and was scared. They must be knowing that her friends had been caught by the police, but what happened with Triparna they would like to know. She wished that her Papa were there to help them, but she hadn't informed any of the parents about all this. She had only told them that they would be staying there for few more days to enjoy the picturesque beauty of Goa. The parents didn't react and asked her to take care. She closed the doors and windows, checked them a number of times and then went to sleep, but she couldn't sleep at all. Lying wide awake, she missed her friends and tried to get many solutions to the problems.

Next morning Loyola reached her place. She hugged Triparna and asked her not to worry. With her sleek brown hair and large eyes that spoke in silence, she dealt with numerous legal cases of a big company that could prove her worth as a lawyer. Her tall figure and confident demeanour made her look like an expert in her field. She called one of her friends who was an eminent lawyer and asked for help. She replied that she would inform the local police station to give them bail and everything would be settled. She requested Loyola to visit the local police station and call her.

Loyola told everything to Triparna. They got ready quickly and headed towards the police station. Loyola called her driver, but his phone number wasn't accessible. Both had a doubt about the driver. Was he involved in drug smuggling? With the duplicate key in her purse, Loyola first told the cab driver to visit the Golden Sands Casino to find out if her car was safe. Within forty-five minutes they reached the place where Triparna and her friends had left the car. They could not find anything there, Triparna felt the ground beneath her feet slipping, as if she was pulled by a certain force under the ground and no trace of her body could be seen anywhere. However, the people there said that police had confiscated the car, and they should go to the local police station. Triparna got a bit relaxed, but she knew that it would be a tough nut to crack.

After half an hour, they reached the police station. Loyola showed her card to the officer- in -charge, and then called her friend.

"Please talk to Ms. Smith, the topmost criminal lawyer of Goa." she said.

"We have come here to get bail for the three girls whom you have arrested in the charge of drug smuggling." she added.

The officer glared at her face asking them to take their seats.

"Do you know Madam what you are talking? How can I leave them without any investigation? They have been caught red-handed with packets of drug carrying in their purses. Isn't it a great offense to the country? You are yourself a lawyer, aren't you? How could you advocate against the law?", he retorted angrily.

"The driver of that red car in which they were travelling is also absconding. You all are in a trap, see?" said he, chewing beetle leaves.

"All right Officer! I know that you have arrested them under Section 13 as they were consuming drug in the casino, but they are completely innocent. They found it in their purse and tried it without knowing anything about it just for fun. You must be knowing how the youngsters are going adventurous nowadays, doing weird things. At least their case is bailable. Now please talk to Ms Smith."

"Well Madam as you know you are not doing anything right, let me talk to Ms. Smith. You and she would be held accountable if anything goes wrong. They will be free to go home but will be house arrested until the hearing of this case is over. We are also putting our best efforts to find out the minds behind this drug trafficking and also the absconding driver."

"Thank you so much Officer!"

"Madam Roma! Let the girls come here. Take them out." he ordered.

"O my dear! How devastated they look!" exclaimed Loyola.

Triparna and Loyola went near the lock-up where they were sitting huddled together.

Hearing Loyola's voice all three rushed and started crying.

"Please please help us. We never intended to take drugs." Sophia said.

"Yes, yes don't worry. You have learnt a lesson now and would act accordingly in future." Loyola said.

Roma, the lady constable, escorted them to the officer. The paperwork was done. They all were free to go.

"May I take my car, Officer? Did you check everything?" Loyola asked.

"Yes, but you also are not allowed to move outside Goa until the case is closed."

"Yes, that I know very well. Thank you for your cooperation, Officer."

"Hariharan! Ask Mohan to bring Madam's car."

The car was brought. They all got inside. Loyola drove the car and went home.

After going home, Olivia, Sophia and Amaya took a bath, had lunch and went to sleep. Triparna and Loyola sat and discussed about the next move. Loyola called Ms. Smith and asked her to fight the case. She agreed.

Next day Ms. Smith came to them and asked everyone about the incident. Then she filed a lawsuit against the owner of the casino where the incident took place. The hearing was after one day. All of them assembled in the court. The owner of the casino was interrogated, and the girls were also questioned. Triparna luckily was not asked to appear in front of the judge. She was in the audience. When they entered the courtroom, the press reporters surrounded them. The barrages of questions were triggered to them. All four tried to hide their identities, but they had become a sensation for the media. All the newspapers flashed their names and stories with photographs. However, Ms. Smith was able to win the case in their favour and they were given a warning of further involvement. The driver, however, was still absconding and the police were vigorously looking for him.

Loyola and all four of them gave a warm hug to Ms. Smith without whose brainy ideas and eloquence they would have never been freed.

Sophia was very emotional and held Loyola like a child who would seek refuge in her mother's bosom. All of them expressed their love and gratitude to her, inviting her to visit Kolkata.

When they came back home, they found hundreds of missed calls from their parents. They were all hesitant to talk to their parents, but they had to. Their parents had watched everything on TV and were fully exhausted.

It was decided that Loyola was going to tell them everything and then the girls would talk to their moms one by one.

First Loyola talked to Olivia's mom as she had not been well when Oli came to Goa for vacation.

"Hello! Aunty how are you? Please listen to me. I am Loyola, Sophia's cousin. Olivia is safe Aunty, and they would leave for Kolkata tomorrow. They were completely innocent and had been trapped. Please be patient. Olivia is fine. Good-bye Aunty! Take care. Please talk to her. Here is she on the phone."

Then Olivia talked to her mom and said she was all right. Her Mom at first scolded her for being so reckless, then pacified her and said they were eagerly waiting for her comeback.

Then Loyola talked to Amaya's Papa and depicted everything. Her Papa was able to comprehend the situation. Then Amaya took the phone and started crying. "I will never be so foolish Papa. Please forgive me." said she, sobbing bitterly. Her parents consoled her and said that she should come home as soon as possible.

Then Loyola talked to Sophia 's mom who broke down and was unable to speak anything. Loyola said, "No more tears Aunty! Everything is fine now. The police are trying to get to the bottom of it and are going to arrest them. Now talk to Sophia." Then Sophia also convinced her mom and said that next day only they would meet, so she must not worry.

Finally, Triparna called her parents.

"Why did you do all this, Tiru? Did I bring you up for this day? I was already thinking that you all were too impulsive and immature. I never thought that to this extent you would have to go. Didn't you ever think of your Papa, how would he feel? A drug inspector's daughter is taking drugs. How can it be dear?" she continued.

"Mom! Please one sec.mom! Please listen to me. I acted as the most mature person amongst us, and it was only me who was stable and hadn't taken anything like drug, rather I threw the packet in the lake and got rid of it. We were completely unaware who and when they kept it in our purses. So please stop blaming me and give the phone to Papa. I will just say "Hello" to him. Tomorrow we would be there by afternoon. Please take care and give the phone to Papa."

"Hello Papa! How are you? Hope you're not misguided like mom. Papa! I am your daughter who has known all ins and outs of this drug abuse. How can I take drug Papa? I always have watched you solving the problems. Of course, at first, I was completely confused, but look we have won and have been able to get out of the game they played. I think the police will catch the gang very soon and then the driver also would be traced. Don't worry Papa! Coming to you tomorrow. Bye!"

"Ok *beta*! You are welcome. I fully understand your predicament. Mommy is like that only. Don't take it personally. Come home. It's high time we visited the park, and my coaching classes are also looking forward to my daughter's coming home. Bye! Happy and safe journey!"

Next morning the final moments arrived. A bittersweet sense of fulfilment and gratitude filled the air. Memories of breathtaking experiences and newfound friendships lingered in the minds of all four as they prepared to bid farewell to their journey and Loyola. Each tale was a testament to their resilience and the lessons learned along the way. Loyola dropped them at the airport. The bonds of friendship were reaffirmed, reminding everyone of the irreplaceable joy found in the cherished companions and the nightmares they had experienced during their stay in Goa.

Three hours forty minutes seemed to be thirty hours as all four of them were exhausted, not looking at each other as if something they had lost forever. How they would meet their parents was the gnawing anxiety that they suffered from. They were oblivious of the circumstances that crackled with energy while starting their journey from Kolkata. However, Triparna tried to lighten up the mood by cracking jokes. They reached Netaji Subhas Chandra Bose International Airport. After collecting their luggage, they headed for the exit gate, hugged each other and were about to find a cab when they were greeted by their parents. It was the precious moment of reunion.

They messaged Loyola that they had arrived safely. They also told her how happy their parents were.

After a few days, their college opened, and they became busy with their daily schedules. Then they got news from Loyola that her driver was found dead near an abandoned building. Police located his family. There was only an old elderly woman who had brought him up, living in a small house in a village. She was childless and had adopted him when he was only six months old. He had fallen in bad company, and she warned him many a times. He was convinced and he tried to get rid of the criminals. The day when the raid was made in the casino, he told the leader that he would no more be in touch with him and would live a normal life. The man laughed and just he had reached the casino, his men kidnapped him. They already had kept the drugs in the purses of the girls inside the casino. Then they stabbed him. Police was still searching for the suspect.

This news filled them with questions about the human mind. Triparna recalled her Papa's observations. "Human mind is like an ocean. There are high tides and low tides. It is really hard to assess what goes on in the mind." The driver had once been tempted to earn money by corrupt means, but when he wished to come back and enjoy a simple life, he was not allowed. Olivia, Amaya and Sophia also could have been victimized by the glamorous world, but they were lucky to get back to their senses and old roots.

They were very much moved, and sincerely they prayed for the departed soul.

Shilpa had listened to the whole story. She just gave a few suggestions to Triparna like an elder sister. She said that human mind is innovative and unparalleled, yet its mysteries remain elusive. However, amidst its complexity lies the essence of humanity that we should never ignore.

Triparna remembered this forever, while solving the problems of mentally unstable people sitting in her clinic.

About the Author

Kajari Guha

Armed with the treasure of decades of experience as an English teacher for the Senior Secondary students of a renowned school of India, Kajari Guha is a published author with great command over English, Bengali and Hindi. She is a poet, translator, musician and composer.

She penned several books for the students of English who would like to improve English language. Memoirs like Bridging the gap-Shatarupa, Don't know Why, Athocho Tumi Udasin, Rangeen, Mahakte Khwab and the stories and poems included in the anthologies like Echoes of Ages, The Lyrics, The Character -Sketch with tiny tales, Yuddh Shastra, Pink, Rick and Pip..the Scuba divers, Born to Thrive, Pinky Mehra's stories published by Ukiyoto, have already garnished the platter of her literary cuisine to captivate even the jaded palates of the readers worldwide. She has translated "Tulsi Ramayana 1008panktite niboddho" from Hindi to Bengali, published from Houston, TX, U.S.A.

www.ingramcontent.com/pod-product-compliance
Lightning Source LLC
LaVergne TN
LVHW041556070526
838199LV00046B/1988